EQUIPPED FOR BATTLE

A 9-Week Study of the Whole Armor of God

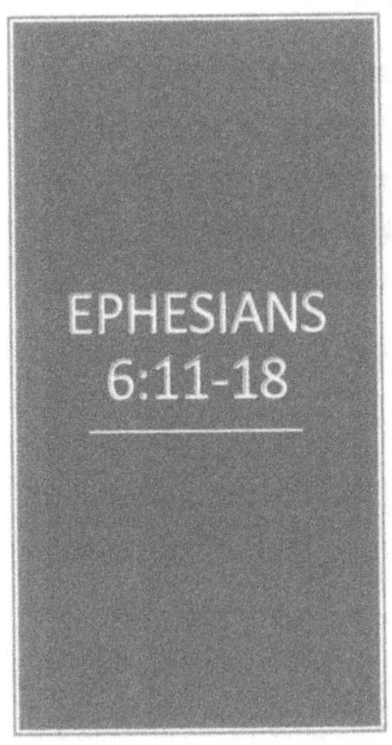

Dr. William Burnham

Dr. William Burnham

Equipped for Battle: A Biblical Study of the Whole Armor of God

A 9-Week Study — Designed for Individuals and Groups

Copyright © 2026 by Dr. William D. Burnham

All rights reserved.

Scripture quotations are taken from the New King James Version® (NKJV®).

Published by:

Just a Thought Ministries

United States of America

Disclaimer

This book is intended for educational and spiritual enrichment purposes only. The author makes no claim that this material replaces personal Bible study, pastoral counsel, or participation in a local church. While care has been taken to ensure theological accuracy, readers are encouraged to study the Scriptures prayerfully and consult trusted biblical resources.

Dedication

[Client will provide details for dedication.]

Acknowledgment

[Client will provide details for acknowledgment.]

Dr. William Burnham

Table of Contents

About the Author

Dr. William D. Burnham has served in pastoral ministry for over forty years as a pastor, teacher, author, and conference speaker. Since 2016, he has faithfully led Tanglewood Community Church in Sebring, Florida. Prior to that, he served for more than two decades as senior pastor of a non-denominational church in Atlanta, Georgia.

Dr. Burnham earned his undergraduate and seminary degrees from Leavell College and New Orleans Baptist Theological Seminary. He later completed both a master's degree in theological studies and a Ph.D. in Communication and Leadership Development from Louisiana Baptist University. His writing ministry reflects a deep commitment to biblical authority, pastoral clarity, and Christ-centered teaching.

The Full Armor Of God

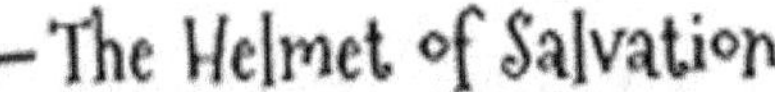

The Helmet of Salvation

Let us be sober, putting on faith and love as a breastplate, and the hope of salvation as a helmet. (1 Thessalonians 5:8, NIV)

The Breastplate of Righteousness

Above all else, guard your heart, for everything you do flows from it. (Proverbs 4:23, NIV)

The Shield of Faith

Resist him, standing firm in the faith, because you know that the family of believers throughout the world is undergoing the same kind of sufferings. (1 Peter 5:9, NIV)

The Belt of Truth

Stand therefore, having your loins girt about with truth. (Ephesians 6:14a, KJV)

The Sword of the Spirit

For the word of God is alive and active. Sharper than any double-edged sword, it penetrates even to dividing soul and spirit, joints and marrow; it judges the thoughts and attitudes of the heart. (Hebrews 4:12, NIV)

Feet Shod With The Preparation of the Gospel of peace

And your feet shod with the preparation of the gospel of peace; (Ephesians 6:15)

♡ Equipped for Battle – Introduction

A Study of the Whole Armor of God

Ephesians 6:10–18

We Are at War

There's no sugarcoating it, if you are a genuine follower of Jesus Christ, you're at war. Not a war with people, political parties, or social movements, but a war in the spiritual realm. The enemy we face is invisible, yet incredibly real. His tactics are subtle, his attacks strategic, and his objective is singular: to destroy everything Christ is building in your life, your home, and your church.

Paul understood this reality when he penned the powerful words found in Ephesians 6:10–18. After laying out in chapters 1–3 the incredible blessings and identity we have in Christ, and then describing in chapters 4–6:9 how Christians ought to live, Paul doesn't end with a benediction, he ends with a battle cry:

"Finally, my brethren, be strong in the Lord and in the power of His might. Put on the whole armor of God, that you may be able to stand against the wiles of the devil." — Ephesians 6:10–11, NKJV

Why? Because the kind of Christian living Paul described is impossible without opposition. If you're living a life filled with God's Spirit and guided by His Word, you can count on spiritual warfare.

Satan Is Real, and So Is the Battle

In a recent study cited in George Barna's What America Believes, nearly half (48%) of those identifying as "born-again Christians" either believed Satan was merely a symbol of evil or weren't sure if he existed at all. That kind of confusion is dangerous. The Bible doesn't leave us in the dark about Satan. He is real, personal, powerful, and utterly opposed to everything God loves.

Here's what Scripture teaches about our adversary:

James 4:7 – "Therefore submit to God. Resist the devil and he will flee from you."

1 Peter 5:8–9 – "Be sober, be vigilant; because your adversary the devil walks about like a roaring lion, seeking whom he may devour. Resist him, steadfast in the faith…"

2 Corinthians 2:11 – "…lest Satan should take advantage of us; for we are not ignorant of his devices."

Acts 20:29–31 – "For I know this, that after my departure savage wolves will come in among you, not sparing the flock… Therefore watch, and remember that for three years I did not cease to warn everyone night and day with tears."

Satan's Strategy Against the Church

In the opening chapters of Revelation (2–3), we're given a unique and sobering glimpse into how Satan attacks Christ's Spirit-filled church. Jesus addresses seven churches in Asia Minor through the pen of the exiled apostle John, who was writing from the island of Patmos. Jesus is seen walking among seven golden lampstands, symbolic of the churches, dressed as Priest, Prophet, and King. He evaluates each church, and His words cut through every façade.

Out of the seven churches:

- Two received no rebuke: Smyrna (persecuted yet pure), Philadelphia (faithful, evangelizing)
- Five received serious warnings: Ephesus (lost love), Pergamum (compromise), Thyatira (tolerance of sin), Sardis (dead religion), Laodicea (lukewarm faith)

These warnings reveal Satan's attacks: cool our love for Christ, invite compromise, tolerate sin, settle for empty activity, and numb us into apathy.

We Can Stand Firm in the Lord's Power

God does not leave His people unprotected. While the devil's power is real, it is limited, and God's power is greater. Every believer has been given a complete suit of spiritual armor, crafted by God Himself.

"Put on the whole armor of God, that you may be able to stand against the wiles of the devil… having done all, to stand." — Ephesians 6:11, 13

You don't have to be a victim. You can resist. You can walk in victory, not in your own strength, but in the Lord's might.

A Call to Prepare

As we begin this study, ask God to open your eyes and strengthen your spirit. The next eight sessions will challenge you, but they will also equip you. God has given you everything you need to walk in spiritual victory, now it's time to put it on and use it.

"The Christian life is not a playground, it's a battleground. But we fight from victory, not for victory." — Warren Wiersbe

Let's get equipped. Let's get serious. Let's stand.

♡ **Equipped for Battle – LESSON ONE**

The Attack Against the Church

Key Passage: Revelation 2–3; Ephesians 6:10–18

Theme: Understanding Satan's strategies against Christ's church and how to stand strong in the armor of God.

Memory Verse: Ephesians 6:10 – "Finally, my brethren, be strong in the Lord and in the power of His might."

Opening Discussion

"What comes to your mind when you hear the phrase 'spiritual warfare'? Can you think of a time when you sensed a spiritual attack?"

____

____

____

____

Read Aloud

- Ephesians 6:10–13
- Revelation 1:9–20 (overview), and then select key verses from Revelation 2–3 (as needed per church below)

"This study begins our series on the armor of God. Before Paul tells us how to stand strong, he reminds us why we must stand strong. In this lesson, we'll explore how Satan attacks churches from within and without, and how Jesus Himself exposes those attacks in Revelation."

Bible Teaching Section – How Satan Attacks the Church

Let's examine each church one at a time. Use the structure below for each church.

1. *Church at Ephesus – The Danger of Losing Your First Love (Rev. 2:1–7)*

Summary Teaching Point: A church can be busy, biblically sound, and doctrinally orthodox, and still be in danger of judgment if love for Christ fades.

Discussion Questions

- What commendations does Jesus give the church at Ephesus?

____

____

____

____

- What did they lose, and how did it affect their ministry?

____

____

____

____

- Why is it dangerous to serve God without love for God?

____

____

____

____

- What does Jesus tell them to do in verse 5, and what might that look like in your life?

____

____

____

____

Personal Reflection

Has your love for Christ cooled? What steps do you need to take to return to your "first love"?

____

____

____

____

2. *Church at Pergamum – The Danger of Compromise (Rev. 2:12–17)*

Summary Teaching Point: Compromise with the world always leads to conflict with the Word.

Discussion Questions

- What made Pergamum such a difficult place to live out the Christian faith?

____

____

____

____

- How did the church begin to compromise?

____

____

____

____

- What modern examples can you think of where the church is compromising with culture?

____

____

____

____

- How does Jesus confront and correct them?

____

____

____

____

Group Application

How do we keep our church from drifting into compromise?

____

____

____

____

3. *Church at Thyatira – The Danger of Tolerating Sin (Rev. 2:18–29)*

Summary Teaching Point: Loving service must never replace holiness. A church can be busy but blind to sin in its ranks.

Discussion Questions

- What good things was this church doing?

____

____

____

____

- What specific sin did Jesus confront?

____

____

____

____

- Why is it dangerous for a church to avoid confronting sin?

____

____

____

____

- What does Jesus mean when He says "I gave her time to repent"? (v. 21)

____

____

____

____

Personal Application

Are there things we are tolerating, either personally or corporately, that Jesus would not tolerate?

____

____

____

____

4. *Church at Sardis – The Danger of Dead Religion (Rev. 3:1–6)*

Summary Teaching Point: A church can have a great reputation, but be spiritually dead.

Discussion Questions

- How does Jesus describe this church's condition?

____

____

____

- What makes a church (or a Christian) appear "alive" on the outside but dead inside?

____

____

____

____

- How can we watch for signs of spiritual apathy in our own lives?

____

____

____

____

Group Challenge

What does it look like to "strengthen what remains" in a dying church?

____

____

____

____

5. *Church at Laodicea – The Danger of Lukewarm Faith (Rev. 3:14–22)*

Summary Teaching Point: Lukewarm Christianity is nauseating to Jesus, it's neither passion nor repentance, just religious self-deception.

Discussion Questions

- Why does Jesus say He will "vomit" this church out?

____

____

____

____

- What made this church blind to its condition?

____

____

____

____

- What four things does Jesus call them to do to return to true spiritual vitality?

____

____

____

____

- What promises are given to those who respond?

____

____

____

____

Personal Reflection

Are you spiritually hot, cold, or lukewarm? What's keeping you from being on fire for Jesus?

____

____

____

____

Wrap-Up and Group Application

Big Idea Recap: Satan's attack on the church follows a pattern:

First Love Lost → Compromise → Tolerating Sin → Dead Religion → Lukewarm Faith

Armor of God Connection

These five attacks show us why we need every piece of spiritual armor from Ephesians 6. In coming lessons, we'll examine how each piece protects us from these kinds of attacks.

Call to Action Step

Ask: "Which of these five attacks do you think our church is most vulnerable to? How can we guard against it together?"

____

____

____

____

Closing Prayer Focus

- That Christ would revive our love
- That we would stay faithful to His Word
- That we would not tolerate sin
- That we would pursue real spiritual life, not just programs
- That we would never become lukewarm

♡ Equipped for Battle – LESSON TWO

The Attack Against the Christian

Key Passage: Ephesians 6:10–13

Theme: Every believer is under daily spiritual attack simply because of who they are in Christ. But God has given us the power, the position, and the provision to stand victorious.

Memory Verse: "Finally, my brethren, be strong in the Lord and in the power of His might." (Ephesians 6:10, NKJV)

Opening Discussion

What are some ways you've experienced spiritual resistance or discouragement since becoming a Christian?

____

____

____

____

The Christian life is not a life of ease. It is a call to arms. Because we are children of God, we are also targets of the enemy. In Ephesians 6:10–13, Paul gives us an urgent call: be strong, be steady, and be smart. God never intended for us to fight spiritual battles in our own strength. Instead, He offers us everything we need to be victorious, because in Christ, the war is already won. But we must be prepared for the daily battle.

Bible Exploration & Discussion

1. Set for the Battle

READ: Ephesians 6:10a; 1 Peter 5:8; Acts 20:28–31

Discussion Questions

- Why do you think Paul ends his letter to the Ephesians with a call to warfare?

____

____

____

____

- How aware are we on a daily basis of the spiritual battles we face?

____

____

____

____

- What does it mean to be spiritually "asleep" to the conflict around us?

____

____

____

____

Application

Write down two practical ways you can begin each day more alert and spiritually prepared.

____

____

____

____

Truth to Remember: The battle is real, and readiness is our first responsibility.

2. *Strength for the Battle*

READ: Ephesians 6:10b; Philippians 4:13; 1 John 4:4; Hebrews 2:14

Discussion Questions

- Why do we often try to face spiritual battles in our own strength?

____

____

____

____

- What does it mean to "be strong in the Lord"? How does that differ from being strong in yourself?

____

____

____

____

- Can you think of a time when God's strength carried you when your own strength failed?

____

____

Application

Identify one area of your life where you need to stop striving in your own strength and start depending on God's power.

Call to Action

Pray daily, asking God to strengthen you by His Spirit before entering the day's battles.

3. *Steady in the Battle*

READ: Ephesians 6:11; Matthew 4:1–11; 2 Corinthians 2:11

Discussion Questions

- What are some of the "wiles" (schemes) Satan uses today to trip up believers?

- Why do we need the "whole" armor and not just a few pieces?

____

____

____

____

- What does it mean to "stand" in spiritual warfare?

____

____

____

____

Activity

List out common spiritual schemes you see affecting Christians today. Share one scheme and how a specific piece of the armor of God would protect against it.

____

____

____

____

Truth to Remember: Satan is subtle, but God has equipped us completely.

4. *Smart in the Battle*

READ: Ephesians 6:12; 2 Corinthians 10:3–5; Luke 23:34

Discussion Questions

- Why is it important to remember that people are not the enemy?

____

____

____

____

- How does misunderstanding our enemy weaken us?

____

____

____

____

- What happens when Christians spend more time fighting each other than standing against the devil?

____

____

____

____

Application

Think of a current conflict in your life. How would it change if you remembered that the person isn't the real enemy?

____

____

____

____

Call to Action

This week, choose to forgive someone who has wronged you and pray for them. Ask God to guard your heart against bitterness.

5. Successful in the Battle

READ: Ephesians 6:13; Romans 8:37; 2 Corinthians 2:14; 1 Corinthians 15:57

Discussion Questions

- What does it look like to "withstand in the evil day"?

- Why is it encouraging to know we fight "from" victory and not "for" victory?

- What is one step you can take to better "stand" your ground spiritually?

Truth to Remember: God has not only equipped you to fight, He has guaranteed your victory in Christ.

Group Challenge

Each member identify one piece of armor they feel least confident about and commit to studying it more in the coming weeks.

Prayer Focus

Ask God to awaken your spiritual senses, strengthen your heart, and help you stand firm in the battles you face this week.

♡ Equipped for Battle – LESSON THREE

The Belt of Truth

Key Passage: Ephesians 6:13–14

Theme: Truth is the foundation of every believer's victory in spiritual warfare. Without it, the rest of the armor cannot be held in place.

Memory Verse: "Stand therefore, having girded your waist with truth, having put on the breastplate of righteousness." (Ephesians 6:14, NKJV)

Opening Discussion

When was a time you believed something that turned out to be false? How did it affect you?

____

____

____

____

In the Roman soldier's armor, the belt held everything else together. Without it, the tunic would flap loose, and weapons would fall away. Paul uses this image to show us how foundational truth is in the Christian life. We live in a world filled with lies, distractions, and deception, but as believers, we are called to be people of truth, grounded in God's Word, committed to living with integrity and spiritual readiness. Truth isn't just what we know, it's who we are and how we live.

Bible Exploration & Discussion

1. *The Battle is Coming*

READ: Ephesians 6:13; 1 Peter 5:8; Revelation 20:10

Discussion Questions

- Why is it important to prepare for spiritual battles before they begin?

- What are some spiritual disciplines that help 'build spiritual muscle' before the fight?

Application

What's one spiritual habit you can strengthen starting this week?

Truth to Remember: Victory begins with preparation.

2. *What Is the Belt of Truth?*

READ: Ephesians 6:14; John 17:17; 2 Timothy 3:16–17

Discussion Questions

- How does God's Word function as truth in our lives?

____

____

____

____

- Why is truth foundational to every other piece of armor?

____

____

____

____

Group Activity

Share one verse or truth from Scripture that has helped you stand firm in a tough season.

3. *Living Girded Lives*

READ: 1 Peter 1:13; Romans 12:1–2; Matthew 16:24

Discussion Questions

- What does it mean to 'gird the loins of your mind'? How do we do that practically?

- What areas of your life need more spiritual discipline and readiness?

Application

Identify one way you will seek to live with greater spiritual integrity this week.

Call to Action

Memorize Ephesians 6:14 and use it as a morning prayer this week.

Closing Reflections

Group Challenge: Each person name one way they want to walk more fully in truth this week, whether by speaking truth, reading truth, or living truth.

Prayer Focus

Ask God to expose any deception in your life and renew your commitment to walk in His truth.

♡ Equipped for Battle – LESSON FOUR

The Breastplate of Righteousness

Key Passage: Ephesians 6:13–14

Theme: Righteousness is not just something we believe; it is how we live. The breastplate of righteousness protects the believer's heart and mind from the enemy's most subtle and dangerous attacks. This practical righteousness is our daily commitment to live holy and obedient lives for God's glory.

Memory Verse: "Stand therefore, having girded your waist with truth, having put on the breastplate of righteousness." (Ephesians 6:14, NKJV)

Opening Discussion

Share a time you forgot something important before heading out for the day (e.g., wallet, phone, keys). What happened?

____

____

____

____

How might forgetting a vital part of your spiritual armor lead to a similar disaster?

____

____

____

____

Napoleon once said, "God is on the side of the strongest battalion," but Scripture disagrees. The Bible shows again and again that God is on the side of those who do right and walk in obedience to Him. Abraham, Gideon, and David all won great victories not because of their numbers, but because of their righteousness and dependence on God. In this lesson, we focus on the breastplate of righteousness, what it means, why it matters, and how we put it on every day.

Bible Exploration & Discussion

READ: Ephesians 6:13–14

1. The Priority of the Breastplate of Righteousness

READ: Proverbs 4:23; Romans 6:13; James 4:7

- Why is righteousness so essential in the believer's daily spiritual life?

____

____

____

____

- What areas of your life does righteousness protect?

____

____

____

____

Group Reflection

Paul's imagery of the breastplate was familiar to his readers...

- How have you experienced spiritual attacks in your mind or emotions recently?

____

____

____

____

- What happens when we don't guard our hearts and minds?

____

____

____

____

Application

List one area of your life where you need to guard your heart more carefully. Share ways to stay spiritually focused when your emotions are under attack.

____

____

____

____

2. *The Protection of the Breastplate of Righteousness*

READ: Job 1:6–7; 2 Corinthians 5:21; Romans 13:12–14

- How does practical righteousness protect us in the spiritual battle?

- Why is holiness so crucial to maintaining spiritual confidence?

Group Insight

We often expect dramatic, "big battles" with the devil...

- What are some common daily battles where righteousness must be our defense?

- How does living righteously impact our ability to resist temptation?

---

3. The Proper Breastplate of Righteousness

READ: Isaiah 64:6; 2 Corinthians 5:17; Philippians 3:4–12

- What's the difference between self-righteousness, imputed righteousness, and practical righteousness?

____

____

____

____

- Why does self-righteousness fail to protect us?

____

____

____

____

Group Exercise

Compare your Christian walk to the practice of a sport or musical instrument...

Reflection

Are you relying on past victories and "church activity" to protect you, or are you actively walking in obedience and holiness each day?

Call to Action

Examine your life:

- Is your heart right with God today?

____

____

____

____

- Is there any unconfessed sin that is weakening your armor?

____

____

____

____

- Are you regularly in God's Word and prayer?

____

____

____

____

Commit to one specific action step this week to walk more righteously:

- Forgive someone
- Speak truth kindly
- Resist temptation with Scripture
- Serve someone selflessly

Prayer Focus

Ask God to:

- Cleanse your heart from hidden sin
- Guard your thoughts and emotions
- Help you wear the breastplate of righteousness every day

Group Challenge

Before next week, spend 15 minutes in quiet time asking God to show you one area where you've let your guard down. Write it down. Bring it back next week to share (if comfortable) how you are seeking to restore that armor piece.

♡ Equipped for Battle – LESSON FIVE

The Gospel Shoes of Peace

Key Passage: Ephesians 6:15

Theme: The Gospel of Peace provides the believer with stability, readiness, and confidence to stand firm against the enemy's attacks. These spiritual shoes ground us in the truth that we are reconciled with God through Christ, and they motivate us to carry the gospel wherever we go.

Memory Verse: "And having shod your feet with the preparation of the gospel of peace." (Ephesians 6:15, NKJV)

Opening Discussion

Share a story of a time you wore the wrong shoes for an activity. What happened?

____

____

____

____

Why do you think Paul compares the gospel to a soldier's boots?

____

____

____

____

In Ephesians 6, Paul uses the imagery of a Roman soldier's armor to describe how believers can stand firm in spiritual warfare. This week, we look at the soldier's shoes, the gospel of peace. Just like military boots equipped Roman soldiers to stand their ground, the gospel gives us firm footing in every battle.

Bible Exploration & Discussion

READ: Ephesians 6:15; Romans 5:1; Isaiah 52:7; 1 Peter 3:15

1. *What These Boots Are Designed For*

READ: Ephesians 6:11, 13–14

- What does it mean to "stand" in the battle?

____

____

____

____

- How do spiritual shoes help us hold ground already won in Christ?

____

____

____

____

Group Insight

Roman soldiers wore hobnailed boots for traction and stability...

Application

What are the "slippery surfaces" you're facing right now where the gospel could give you firmer footing?

____

____

____

____

2. *Why These Boots Are Desired*

READ: Colossians 1:11–14; Philippians 4:7; Romans 10:15

- How does the gospel bring peace to your life amid chaos?

____

____

____

____

- Why does every believer need "readiness" from the gospel?

____

____

____

____

Reflection

Many own gospel shoes but never wear them, what prevents Christians from standing confidently in the peace of Christ?

____

____

____

____

<u>Application</u>

Identify areas where you are not currently living with gospel readiness.

____

____

____

____

3. *What These Boots Depict*

READ: Titus 3:1; Acts 1:8; Matthew 28:18–20

- What does Paul mean by "preparation" in Ephesians 6:15?

____

____

____

____

- How does gospel peace prepare us for witness and spiritual conflict?

____

____

____

____

Group Exercise

Practice sharing a one-minute version of your salvation testimony.

4. What These Boots Deliver

READ: Romans 5:1–11; 2 Chronicles 20:15–23; Judges 7:15–22

- What stories from Scripture show how peace with God leads to confidence and victory?

____

____

____

____

- How does gospel peace impact the way you respond to spiritual attack?

____

____

____

____

Reflection

When facing battle, are you operating from a place of gospel peace or spiritual fear?

____

____

____

____

Call to Action

This week:

- Reflect on your standing with God. Are you confident in your salvation?

____

____

____

____

- Walk in gospel peace. Take steps to live out your faith with boldness and confidence.

____

____

____

____

- Look for one opportunity to share your testimony or the gospel with someone.

____

____

____

____

Prayer Focus

Ask God to:

- Strengthen your foundation in the gospel
- Fill your heart with His peace
- Prepare your feet to bring the good news to others

Group Challenge

Before next week, write out a simple 3-part testimony:

1. Your life before Christ
2. How you came to Christ.
3. Your life since.

Be ready to share it with someone who needs peace.

♡ **Equipped for Battle – LESSON SIX**

The Shield of Faith

Key Passage: Ephesians 6:16

Theme: Faith is more than belief, it is trust in the power and promises of God in the face of attack. The shield of faith is our defense against the enemy's fiery darts of temptation, doubt, fear, and deception. When we stand behind the shield of faith, we declare that God is our defender and His Word is our truth.

Memory Verse: "Above all, taking the shield of faith with which you will be able to quench all the fiery darts of the wicked one." (Ephesians 6:16, NKJV)

Opening Discussion

Share a time you were caught off guard or unprepared for something. What helped you make it through?

____

____

____

____

Why do you think Paul says to take up the shield of faith "above all" other armor pieces?

____

____

____

____

Paul calls faith a shield because our trust in God is what protects us when life's battles intensify. Satan launches attacks to weaken us, through fear, temptation, doubt, and lies. But God has given us the shield of faith, which, when raised, deflects every flaming arrow of the enemy.

Bible Exploration & Discussion

READ: Ephesians 6:10–16; Hebrews 11:6; Psalm 3:3–4

1. *How the Shield of Faith is Designed*

READ: Proverbs 30:5–6; Psalm 18:30; 2 Samuel 22:31

- What kind of shield did Roman soldiers use?

____

____

____

____

- What protection did it offer?

____

____

____

____

- How does understanding the Roman shield help us picture faith's function in our lives?

____

____

____

____

Group Insight

Like the Roman phalanx, believers together form a wall of defense when united in faith. How does shared faith protect the church as a body?

____

____

____

____

Application

What are some 'fiery darts' you've experienced this week (e.g., fear, shame, anger)? How did faith help, or how can it help next time?

____

____

____

____

2. *How the Shield of Faith is Described*

READ: Hebrews 11:1–6; Romans 1:17; Ephesians 2:8–9

- What does it mean to live by faith every day, not just at salvation?

____

____

____

____

- Why is faith more than belief, it is action and trust?

____

____

____

____

Reflection

Charles Spurgeon said, "Believe this book of God, every letter of it…" do you believe every word of Scripture with that kind of faith?

____

____

____

____

3. *How the Shield of Faith is Deployed*

READ: 1 John 5:4; Matthew 4:1–11; Genesis 3:1–6

- How does Satan launch his fiery darts against us today?

____

____

____

____

- How did Jesus respond to Satan's attacks in Matthew 4?

____

____

____

____

- What does that teach us about deploying faith?

____

____

____

____

Group Exercise

In pairs, write down a fiery dart Satan has used against you and then find a Scripture promise to raise as your shield.

____

____

____

____

Call to Action

This week:

- List areas where you are vulnerable to attack and commit them to God in faith.

____

____

____

____

- Memorize one scripture that strengthens your trust in God's promises.

- Encourage someone else in the group this week by reminding them of God's faithfulness.

Prayer Focus

Ask God to:

- Strengthen your shield of faith daily
- Help you trust Him even when the path is unclear
- Quench every fiery dart through your dependence on His Word

Group Challenge

Create a 'Faith Shield' board this week. Write down lies Satan uses against you on one side and truths from Scripture to counter them on the other. Bring one to share.

♡ Equipped for Battle – LESSON SEVEN

The Helmet of Salvation

Key Passage: Ephesians 6:17a

Theme: The Helmet of Salvation is essential for protecting the believer's mind from the devil's dual-edged broadsword, discouragement and doubt. This lesson helps believers understand how assurance in Christ guards their thoughts and gives them the strength to remain steadfast in spiritual warfare.

Memory Verse: "And take the helmet of salvation..." (Ephesians 6:17a, NKJV)

Opening Discussion

Why is protecting your mind so crucial in your Christian walk? What dangers do we face when we "forget our helmet"?

____

____

____

____

Many Christians today fail to 'mind their heads.' Surrounded by worldly thinking and shallow doctrine, their minds become vulnerable to Satan's attacks. Paul calls us to 'take the helmet of salvation', an act that guards our minds with assurance, sound thinking, and eternal security. In this lesson, we explore how the helmet protects us from discouragement and doubt, helping us hold our ground in the spiritual battle.

Bible Exploration & Key Truths

1. The Helmet Provides Protection

READ: Ephesians 6:17; 2 Corinthians 10:3–5; Romans 12:1–2

Why is your mind a primary battlefield in spiritual warfare? What happens when it's unguarded?

____

____

____

____

Insight

The Roman helmet deflected death blows. Spiritually, assurance in salvation protects the mind from Satan's attempts to destroy confidence and trust in Christ.

2. The Helmet Guards Against Discouragement

READ: 1 Kings 19:1–18 (Elijah); Job 13:15; Psalm 73

Group Questions

- How has discouragement affected your walk with God?

____

____

- Why does discouragement make us spiritually vulnerable?

Elijah's discouragement came after major victory. Job, though devastated, still trusted God. We too must guard our minds from the lies that follow trials and setbacks.

3. *The Helmet Guards Against Doubt*

READ: John 10:28–29; Romans 8:38–39; Philippians 1:6; 1 Peter 1:3–5; 2 Timothy 1:12

<u>*Questions for Reflection*</u>

- Have you ever struggled with doubts about your salvation?

- How does Scripture assure you of your secure position in Christ?

____

____

Discussion

Satan loves to attack assurance. The helmet protects against lies that make us question God's love, forgiveness, and saving power.

Practical Application

- Examine your salvation (2 Corinthians 13:5; 2 Peter 1:10)
- Write down three truths from Scripture that assure you of your salvation

____

____

____

____

- When you feel discouraged or doubtful this week, read them aloud and thank God for His promise

Call to Action & Prayer Focus

Pray together:

Thank God for the helmet of salvation

Ask God to protect your mind from discouragement and doubt

Pray for others in your group to be rooted in assurance

Group Challenge

Memorize one verse this week that strengthens your confidence in Christ (e.g., Romans 8:38–39 or John 10:28). Share next week how that truth helped you resist discouragement or doubt.

♡ Equipped for Battle – LESSON EIGHT

The Sword of the Spirit

Key Passage: Ephesians 6:17–18

Theme: The Word of God is the only offensive weapon in the believer's spiritual arsenal. As the sword of the Spirit, it cuts through deception, defeats temptation, and drives the enemy back. This lesson helps believers understand how to use Scripture skillfully in spiritual warfare through prayerful application and bold proclamation.

Memory Verse: "And take the helmet of salvation, and the sword of the Spirit, which is the word of God." (Ephesians 6:17, NKJV)

Opening Discussion

Share a time you used the right tool for the job. What difference did it make?

____

____

____

____

How might using the wrong spiritual tool, or not using one at all, leave you vulnerable in spiritual battles?

____

____

Every piece of armor we've studied so far is defensive. Only one is offensive: the sword of the Spirit. Paul makes it clear, this weapon is the Word of God. Used in combination with Spirit-led prayer, this sword has divine power to defeat the enemy. Today, we'll explore how to wield this sword skillfully and confidently.

Bible Exploration & Key Truths

1. *The Identity of the Sword*

READ: Ephesians 6:17; 2 Timothy 3:16–17; Hebrews 4:12

- What does Paul mean by "the sword of the Spirit?"

- Why is the Bible our only offensive weapon?

Insight

The Greek word for "sword" here refers to the short dagger (machaira), designed for close combat. Paul uses the term "rhema" (utterance) for 'word,' indicating the precise, Spirit-led application of Scripture during spiritual battles.

2. *The Importance of the Sword*

READ: Matthew 4:1–11; Deuteronomy 6:13, 16; Deuteronomy 8:3

- How did Jesus use Scripture to defeat Satan's temptations?

____

____

____

____

- What does this teach us about the power of the Word in real life situations?

____

____

____

____

Application

Memorizing Scripture is not just a discipline, it's a spiritual strategy. Like Jesus, we need to know specific verses for specific struggles. The sword of the Spirit is powerful when applied directly to the enemy's lies.

3. *The Impact of the Sword and Prayer*

READ: James 4:7; Psalm 119:11; Philippians 4:6–7; Hebrews 4:16

- How does pairing God's Word with prayer empower us to stand?

____

____

____

____

- Why is prayer essential in effectively using the Word?

____

____

____

____

<u>Insight</u>

R.A. Torrey taught that prayer is God's appointed means to resist Satan, receive grace, and experience peace. When the Word fills our mind and prayer directs our heart, we are spiritually unstoppable.

Practical Application & Group Discussion

- What verse has personally helped you resist temptation?

____

____

____

____

- What Scripture do you need to memorize for your current battle?

____

____

____

____

- What spiritual "ground" has God given you that the enemy is trying to take?

____

____

____

____

Call to Action & Prayer Focus

This week:

Choose one verse to memorize and meditate on daily.

Pray it aloud each morning and evening.

Ask the Spirit to help you use it when spiritual attack comes.

Prayer

Thank God for the power of His Word

Ask for discernment to speak the right verse at the right time

Pray for boldness to share Scripture in spiritual conversations

♡ **Equipped for Battle – LESSON NINE**

Standing Strong: Final Encouragements for Victory

Key Passage: Ephesians 6:10

Theme: As we come to the conclusion of our study on the armor of God, we are reminded that spiritual warfare is not a one-time battle but a lifelong campaign. Victory comes not by our own strength, but by standing strong in the power of the Lord, fully equipped with His armor, grounded in His Word, and guided by prayer. This final session challenges us to live out what we've learned and keep standing, courageously, consistently, and prayerfully.

Memory Verse: "Finally, my brethren, be strong in the Lord and in the power of His might." (Ephesians 6:10, NKJV)

Opening Discussion

- What has been your biggest takeaway from this study?

\
\
\

- Why do you think Paul ends his letter with the call to "stand?"

____

____

____

____

Scripture Reflections & Final Encouragements

1. *Keep Standing*

READ: Ephesians 6:10–14; 1 Corinthians 16:13

- What does "standing" look like in your daily walk?

____

____

____

____

- How can you remain unshaken when life's battles intensify?

____

____

____

____

Reflection

Standing isn't passive. It's active, deliberate, and determined. It means holding the line, refusing to retreat, and keeping our eyes on Jesus. We stand because God has already won the war, we're simply claiming His victory.

2. *Keep Praying*

READ: Ephesians 6:18; Philippians 4:6–7; Colossians 4:2

* Why is prayer essential in spiritual warfare?

____

____

____

____

* What does it look like to pray "at all times" in your life?

____

____

____

____

Insight

Prayer is not our backup plan, it's our battle plan. It's how we draw strength, receive guidance, and maintain connection with our Commander.

3. *Keep Growing*

READ: 2 Peter 3:18; Hebrews 5:12–14; Psalm 1:1–3

* What habits help you grow spiritually?

____

____

____

____

* Where is God calling you to grow stronger next?

____

____

____

____

Encouragement

Armor is meant to be worn daily. Spiritual growth doesn't happen by accident, it's the result of consistent time in God's Word, obedience in action, and walking in community with other believers.

Group Discussion & Testimony Sharing

- Share one way you've seen spiritual growth since beginning this study.

____

____

____

____

- How has your understanding of spiritual warfare changed?

____

____

____

____

- What "piece of armor" has meant the most to you, and why?

____

____

Call to Action & Prayer Focus

This week:

- Reflect on the full armor of God (Ephesians 6:10–18).
- Write a personal commitment to wear each piece daily.

- Choose one person to encourage or disciple in their spiritual walk.

Prayer Focus

Thank God for equipping you with everything needed for victory.

Ask for spiritual alertness and perseverance.

Pray for fellow believers who are facing intense battles.

Final Challenge

You are equipped for battle. The enemy is real, but so is your Savior. Walk boldly, wear your armor daily, wield your sword wisely, and stay connected through prayer. Victory is not just possible, it's promised. Now go, stand strong in the Lord and in the power of His might!